th
X
sh
Th
x
Y
ch
Sh
y
Ch
This is Boxfish.
I0816733

Boxfish is meeting Shrimp for lunch.

A rock has cracked Crab's shell.

Boxfish fixes Crab's shell with string.

Thanks, Boxfish!
Must dash!

Eel is stuck in thick weeds.

Boxfish helps Eel.
Eel is free!

Thanks, Boxfish!
Boxfish swims on in a rush.

Boxfish sees his chum, Shrimp.

But Haddock's Shack is shut!

Boxfish and Shrimp cannot have lunch!

Just then, Crab and Eel swim along with sandwiches for Boxfish.